OUR

BROKEN

EARTH

DEMITRIA LUNETTA

An imprint of Enslow Publishing

WEST **44** BOOKS™

Please visit our website, www.west44books.com.
For a free color catalog of all our high-quality books,
call toll free 1-800-542-2595 or fax 1-877-542-2596.

Cataloging-in-Publication Data

Names: Lunetta, Demitria.
Title: Our broken Earth / Demitria Lunetta.
Description: New York : West 44, 2022.
Identifiers: ISBN 9781978595408 (pbk.) | ISBN 9781978595392
(library bound) | ISBN 9781978595415 (ebook)
Subjects: LCSH: Poetry, American--21st century. | English poetry. |
Young adult poetry, American. | Poetry, Modern--21st century.
Classification: LCC PS586.3 O974 2022 | DDC 811'.60809282--dc23

First Edition

Published in 2022 by
Enslow Publishing LLC
29 East 21st Street
New York, NY 10011

Editor: Caitie McAneney
Designer: Seth Hughes

Photo Credits: Cover (bear) Lesya Pogosskaya/Shutterstock.com;
cover (ground) Mia Stendal/Shutterstock.com; cover (sky)
Vasin Lee/Shutterstock.com; cover (cityscape) Designer things/
Shutterstock.com; cover (rain) railway fx/Shutterstock.com.

Printed in the United States of America

CPSIA compliance information: Batch #CS22W44: For further information contact
Enslow Publishing LLC, New York, New York at 1-800-542-2595.

<u>1</u>

The earth hates us.

With its rising tides
                        and poison winds
                                        and angry sun
                                                        and toxic rain.

It's raining now.

None of us dare to brave the storm.

Not for anything.

2

"Mal!"

Kurtis screams.
    He's two years younger than me.
    Fourteen, but small for his age.

"The rain! It's getting in!"

There's a leak and the unpleasant stuff drips down.

Kurt panics, but
I grab a metal bucket.
    Rusted.
    Worn out.
    Broken.

Like everything here.

3

We huddle inside the

    one room that we call ours.

    One room in an apartment with ten.

    One room in a building with hundreds.

    One room in a block with thousands.

Jaynee tells me that

    one family used to live in each apartment in
    this industrious, expensive, seaside city.

It feels like a lie. It is too much space for one family.

But…

4

Jaynee knows
   things.

Jaynee knows
   that there used to be more land.

Jaynee knows
   that it was not always this hot.

Jaynee knows
   the water that falls from the sky wasn't
   always bad.

To walk in.
To bathe in.
To drink without it
   burning your throat and
   turning your insides to mush.

<u>5</u>

I watch the rain

   drip

into the bucket.

And
   with each drop, the foul water splashes a little
   onto the rim.

And
   soon it will eat through the worn wooden floor.

And
   we will fall through to the family beneath.

And
   we will have nowhere to go.

The rain drips down.

d   d   d   d

r   r   r   r

i   i   i   i

p   p   p   p

Did the earth always hate us?

Jaynee's sleeping now, but I'll ask her when she wakes.

<u>7</u>

Jaynee tells us:

Once the earth was not broken.
But we hurt it.
Used it.
Trashed it.

So now it is paying us back.
Killing us.
Quickly with violent storms.
Slowly with poison water.

Even before I lost it all,
I had never known
the earth to be kind.

But I guess it has a reason
for all the heartbreak
it brings to us.

All of us have lost people.
Jaynee, Kurt, Tia, Garret, Skye,
and me—Malcolm. Mal.
I lost my entire family when the earth sent a flood.
Mom. Dad. My sister.
I was only ten years old.

We had a small house on the Florida panhandle.
We ate rations from boxes and cans and jars.
We drank bottle after bottle of water.
We had strong walls and windows.

We thought we were
far from the sea.
But we weren't far enough.

The water rushed in and we spilled out.
I grabbed for my sister's hand,
but it slipped through my fingers.

Then there was blackness.
I woke and coughed up the whole sea.
My lungs burned as I vomited water.
I passed out again.

I woke alone.
No mom.
No dad.
No sister.
They were all gone.

I walked the shoreline,
once so far, but now so close,
and discovered others.
Other people who had nobody.

Jaynee was first – a girl a few years older than me.
She helped me when I'd lost everything.
And then we found the rest of them.
Over time, we made our own family.

Jaynee is the smart one. The oldest of us.
    She knows things, and
        when she doesn't, she learns things.

Garret is the funny one. Large and goofy.
    He always has a joke and
        makes us all laugh, even when we're down.

Tia is the strong one. Thin but with an inner strength.
    She keeps us going and
        never lets us quit, even when life seems darkest.

Kurt is the soft one. Sensitive. A few years younger
than me.
    He wears his emotions like a coat, and
        it keeps us from getting too hard, too cold.

Skye is the youngest. She's only seven.
    She's weak and sick, and
        we all love her the most.

Me?

Who am I?

Malcolm, the...

smart?
strong?
sensitive?
funny?
weak?

I'm just me.

And I'm not sure that's enough.

Skye is sick.
She clutches her purple teddy bear as
her cough shakes the room and
her breath rattles in her chest.

Cough

Cough

Cough

Skye used to laugh, but now she only coughs.

10

Jaynee says, "Mal. We have to leave this place.

We must go north.
>Where there is a sea of fresh water.
>Where the rain isn't poison
>and the air isn't evil.

We must go
>where the world
>is not yet broken."

Does such a place really exist?

11

The rain has finally stopped

    falling.

Jaynee and I look at each other,

    worried.

We must go grab our food before it all

    disappears.

This is the most dangerous time.

<u>12</u>

Kurt hates to leave the building.
He volunteers to stay with Skye.
    The two smallest of our group.
    They huddle together.
    Kurt's scared.
    We're all scared.
    Of what's waiting for us.

Out there.

Jaynee, Tia, Garret, and I must go look.

We wrap cloth around our faces.
We tuck our pants into our socks.
We wear gloves and shoes lined with plastic.

We face the earth.

13

The beach is shorter than it was before the storm.
  The white sand is covered in dead fish—
      rotting
      stinking
      foul.

If only we could eat those.
    (I gag at the thought.)

The air is hazy.
    (I squint through the mist.)

The sun is orange.
The sky is purple.
The sea is black.

<u>14</u>

We search the beach.

Things always wash up after it rains.

    Tia finds a sheet of plastic.
        It will help fix the hole in the roof.

    Jaynee finds a live creature.
        She says it is a crab and we can eat it.

    I find nothing.
        But…

    Garret finds a box filled with food
        wrapped in plastic.
        Military rations
        meant to last for years.

    I am so happy I almost cry.

15

There are other searchers
    on the beach.
We try to hide our haul.

But it takes the four of us to carry the box of food.

Jaynee covers it
    with the plastic sheet
but people notice.

They start to gather around us.

They try to see
    what we have found
and if they can take it from us.

We are going to have to fight.

<u>16</u>

"Run!" I yell.

And we do.
But hands reach for us.

    I kick.

    I scream.

    I punch.

    I spit.

I bleed.

17

Jaynee is smarter.

> She spots a group from our building.
> "Help us, we will share!" she yells to them.

> They surround us.
> Guard us.
> Protect us.

When we are safe inside our building,
> Jaynee gives them half.

Kurt grumbles.
> But Jaynee is right.

Half is better than none.

18

Jaynee looks at the cut on my face
    and dabs it with clean water.

pain   pain   pain

There's a rip on my glove,
    and some of the poison seawater touched my skin.

pain

        pain

            pain

It itches, but I know better than to scratch.
    It will get worse and rotten if I don't take care of it.

pain

pain

pain

It hurts.
    But I've had worse.

pain   **pain**   **pain**

When Jaynee finishes with
my cuts and bruises,
she yells at me.

"Mal, you are an idiot!"

I should have told her about my glove rip first.

My hand is even redder,
even more itchy,
even more painful.

I breathe through it so I don't scratch.

I don't want boils
that will grow and burst
and ooze green pus.

It's happened before.

I soak my hand in the clean water,
grateful that the apartment gets its water
from under the ground.

The bad water goes down,
through dirt and sand and rock
and the poison gets left behind.
It pumps back up clean enough.

That's why so many people live here.

That's why we live here,
but Jaynee says the clean water will not last forever.
I don't think anything will last forever.

Not even the earth.

Kurt and Tia sort all the remaining food so we know what we have and how long it will last.

24 packets of beef stew
48 packets of peanut butter
24 packets of spaghetti and meatballs
48 protein bars
96 packets of crackers
48 cheese packets
48 chocolate bars

21

I wrap my hand in a clean cloth
and stare at the food.

My stomach growls low
and loud.

Jaynee pulls out one beef stew packet
and puts the rest away.

We have to save what we have
and always plan ahead.

Otherwise the food will run out
and we will starve.

22

Kurt heats the beef stew on the stove.

We all gather around, inhaling the scent.

Tia puts out the bread she baked before we found our haul.

Bread that would have alone been our dinner.

The stew smells so good Skye begins to cry.

We all know how she feels.

23

We have a feast!

We rip
through
bread
and
eat.

Even little Skye,

still
sick
and
coughing,
eats.

<u>24</u>

"I'm going to tell you a story," Jaynee says.

"Of the Shining City, by the lake?" Skye asks.

It's her favorite.
It's *our* favorite.

Jaynee lights a candle and we all
gather around it, making a circle on the floor.

Tia throws us pillows and Skye leans against Garret.
We make ourselves comfortable.

<u>25</u>

Once upon a time,
there was a Shining City by a lake.

The lake was clear and pure,
And healthy fish swam in its waters.

"What made the city shine?" Skye asks,
though she's heard this story a hundred times.

The city shone because it had
unlimited electricity.

Thousands of lights lit the dark night
and kept the cold away.

Once upon a time, there lived
a girl in the Shining City.

But her parents were wicked,
and they were forced to leave.

"What did they do?" Skye asks,
and Kurt shushes her.

What they did isn't important.
What's important is they had to leave the Shining City.

And journey to a place where
everything is dead or dying.

26

My eyes get heavy as Jaynee talks.

The Shining City sounds amazing.
Everyone there is safe and protected.

It must be a fairy tale, because why would anyone
ever do anything that would risk that?

Still, I like to listen, and I begin to doze off as
Jaynee talks about traveling to the Shining City
on a train.

With a full belly, surrounded by my family,
I fall asleep happy.

27

"The water is rising,"
Jaynee whispers to me in the morning.

"We have to leave, Mal."

"Soon this building will be underwater,"
Jaynee tells me.

"Mal, we have to leave."

"We must go north where the water is clean,"
Jaynee says.

"We have to leave, Mal."

"Skye is too sick to survive in this place,"
Jaynee pleads.

"Mal, we have to leave."

Am I strong enough to leave?

Jaynee pulls out a map, old and yellowing.

"We are here," she points. The Florida Panhandle.
"We must go here." Lake Michigan.

It will take months.

Her finger moves up the page.

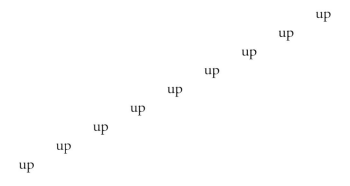

The map makes it seem close, but it really is so very far.

"What is this?" I ask.

> "That is where the land used to be
> before the water swallowed it up."

"What is this?" I ask.

> "That is where we are now,
> on the edge of the world."

"What is this?" I ask.

> "That is the path we must take
> to go north."

"What is this?" I ask.

> "That is where we will end up
> in a city by a lake."

"What is this?" I ask.

> "That is a lake of fresh water
> as big as the ocean."

"What is this?" I ask.

> "That is our only hope
> at a real life."

30

I tell the others that we cannot stay.

We have to go to this new city—
it may not be the Shining City,
but it is our only hope to live.

> Jaynee smiles sadly.
>> She convinced me.

> Garret nods.
>> He is with us.

> Kurt frowns.
>> He is afraid.

> Tia shakes her head.
>> She does not want to go.

> Skye coughs in her bed.
>> I will carry her if I have to.

It is decided.
We will go.

31

Before the basement of the building flooded months ago,
Jaynee looted it for supplies.

Useless things that we all thought just took up space,
but Jaynee had her reasons.

Garret joked that Jaynee had lost her mind,
but no one laughed.

Now we realize Jaynee knew that we would one day
need suitcases with wheels and warmer clothes and
empty plastic bottles.

We pack up all the food
and as much water as we can.

Skye wants her purple teddy bear and we let her keep
it. No one has the heart to say no, and it's not heavy.

32

We wrap what we can in plastic.

We wrap ourselves in plastic.

We wrap our hopes in plastic.

33

Tia is not coming.

> She tells us with tears in her eyes.
> She tells us that she thinks we will all die on the road.
> She tells us we're foolish.
> She tells us she can't just leave.

She hugs herself with her thin arms.

I thought if anyone would stay, it would be Kurt,
who is always so afraid.

We are all so afraid.

34

I'm sad that Tia isn't coming,
    but I can't make her.

Just like I can't make the sea stay low
    or make Skye stop coughing
    or give Kurt courage
    or fix this broken earth.

Jaynee is smart.

She invited others.

A brother and sister from the group that helped us that day on the beach.

Rob and Rowan.

They are tall and quiet.

They are strong and fierce.

They will help us reach the north.

Jaynee is smart.

36

We say goodbye to Tia.
    She looks miserable,
    but she's determined to stay.

Most everyone cries.
    Even me.
    I'm not ashamed.

Garret pretends not to.
    He covers his face and jokes
    that there's something in his eye.

Skye doesn't understand.
　　She tells Tia we'll meet her at the Shining City.
　　She doesn't know it's not *real*.

Jaynee is stone-faced.
　　I squeeze her hand.
　　She feels responsible.

We all love Tia.
　　She's our family.
　　I hope she finds a new family soon.

Family is everything.
　　You can't survive without it.
　　You can't survive in this world alone.

37

Walking away from the building is hard.
    There's a road, but it's crumbling.

The wheels of the suitcase snag as I pull it.
    The plastic crinkles and flaps.

We pass buildings that have collapsed.
    Trees are yellowed and rotting.

Cars are abandoned everywhere.
    Rusted and useless.

Any building that is whole
    has people inside.

They stare at us with wide eyes.
    Hateful or hopeful?

I can't tell.

38

Besides the two new members to our group,
    I'm the largest and Garret is next.
    We take turns carrying Skye.

She weighs less than a feather.

She weighs nothing at all.

But to carry her feels heavy.

Heavy in my heart.
Heavy in my mind.
Heavy in my soul.

Because she weighs nothing at all.

<u>39</u>

Jaynee tells us when to stop and when to go.
Jaynee tells us when to eat and how much.
Jaynee tells us when to hide and when to run.
Jaynee tells us who can sleep and who must watch.

Without Jaynee, we would be lost.

40

I still miss Tia,
but Rowan and Rob are okay.

They carry their share and take their turns to watch.

They listen to Jaynee,
and Rob offers to carry Skye for a while.

Garret and Kurt don't talk to them much.
They stay together.
They don't trust them.

But I like them.
Especially Rowan.

41

I noticed Rowan a while back,
when she and her brother were with that other group.

Her eyes are bright and her laugh is joyful.
Thinking of her always makes me feel warm.

She has strong legs and long black hair.
Hair that grows up and out and frames her face.

Garret joked once that she looked like a wild woman.
Like you didn't know if she would kiss you or punch you.

I think she looks like a dream.
I think she is perfect.

42

My legs are sore from walking the torn-up road,
    past crumbling bridges and buildings.
    My shoulders hurt from lugging my suitcase
        over bumps.
When we finally stop for the night,
    we make camp in whatever rubble we find.
    Every night is the same, but different.
I am asleep as soon as my head touches the ground.

When it is my turn
    to watch,
I stand so that I don't
    accidentally fall asleep.
I would die before I let my family down.

It's been five days without rain.

    We've been lucky.

But we keep everything covered.

    We keep plastic on us.

We will see if it is enough, the first time it rains.

<u>44</u>

The sun
        beats down
                on us.

I want
        to shed
                my clothes.

But the
        layers keep
                us safe.

The sun
        can burn
                and scar.

I decide
        to take
                the heat.

I notice that Rowan is walking beside me.
She's as tall as I am.
I like that.

"Mal, are you worried?" she starts to ask.
She stops and looks at the ground.
At her boots.
At the sky.

"Are you worried that there is no place
better than where we were?"

It's all I think about.
All the time.
That we will walk forever.
And never find a home.

"No," I tell her. "Jaynee is always right."
She smiles at me and I grin back.

Then the rain starts.

46

A fat raindrop
    falls on my arm
        and splashes off the plastic.

Kurt screams
    and I run to him,
        try to calm him down.

There's no shelter,
    but Jaynee prepared for this.
        Made us practice.

She pulls out her tent
    but there's no time to
        set it up properly.

Instead she tosses it out
    like a net and opens the flap.
        We practiced this too.

We crawl inside,
    and it's like we are just
        supplies thrown hurriedly into a bag.

There's no structure,
    so I stand and hold up the middle
        so everyone can get settled.

Jaynee comforts Kurt
    while Garret has Skye.
        Rowan and Rob sit at my feet.

Skye managed to grab her purple teddy bear
    and clutches it to her chest,
        humming a soft lullaby.

I sit down and sigh,
    and Rowan's hand finds mine
        and squeezes.

Rowan begins to hum with Skye
    and soon we all sing along.
        It helps relieve the tension.

We all huddle together
    as close as we can
        and wait out the storm.

<u>47</u>

It rains all night.

The tent smells like too many people
   in too small a space.

We left our suitcases outside the tent.
We left our clean water in our suitcases.
We sleep because there is nothing else to do.

<u>48</u>

In the morning,
the sun dries the rain
and we are lucky
that only one suitcase
was washed away.

We gather everything together
and sip some water
and each have a cracker
with peanut butter
and continue on our way.

In the afternoon,
we stop to rest and
eat some cold spaghetti
and nobody talks.
We are so beat.

Then Rowan and Rob
begin to sing
a song I've never heard
about traveling on a long road
with no end in sight.

Skye watches them
with wonder in her eyes
and I feel the same
because the music
is beyond beautiful.

It always surprises me
how there can be
little bits of beauty
stuck in the cracks
of a barren landscape.

In the evening, we stop
for the night and
have a sip of water
and some stale bread
and beef stew.

Skye coughs and
refuses to drink or eat,
even when Jaynee passes
around some chocolate—
one square each.

Rowan enjoys her
chocolate so much,
I offer her my square
and blush when she
places it on her tongue.

49

That night, there is a sound in the darkness.
    A sound I almost remember.
    A sound I can't place.

We look to Jaynee
    to tell us what it is.
    She always has all the answers.

And she tells us it's a bird.
    One that must have survived.
    One that sings at night.

That starts an argument.

"There are no birds,"
    Kurt says.

"They're all dead,"
    Rob agrees.

"It must be a mutant,"
    Garret jokes.

"Something new, that sounds like a bird,"
    Rowan agrees.

"It's a bird,"
    Skye says, her voice hopeful.

"It's a bird,"
    I agree.

Then no one has the heart to say any different.

We've been lucky.

> The rain has been light.
> The roads have been clear.
> There has been no one else.

We've been lucky.

Too lucky.

But now our luck has run out.

51

When the bandits attack,
I don't understand what's happening.

When the bandits attack,
I look on dumbly.

When the bandits attack,
I let one take my suitcase, not understanding.

When the bandits attack,
I am useless.

52

Jaynee screams, "Circle up!"

She keeps her head, even in the mess.

We've practiced this, and finally I feel my feet moving.

Into my position.

I let them take my suitcase without a fight,

but they will get no more.

We form a circle with the other suitcases piled
in the middle.

Skye sits on top.

Rob screams, "Fight for what's ours!"

Jaynee has a rusty knife.
Kurt has a letter opener.
Garret has a baseball bat.
Rowan has an old piece of jagged metal.
Rob has a wooden board with a nail.

I have a metal pipe that I hold before me like a sword.

53

There are five bandits.
    They are all adults.
    Thin and covered in sores.

They look like a strong wind could break them.
    But they also look mean
    and determined.

They come at us.
    I strike with my metal pipe,
    barely daring to look.

It connects with someone's arm,
    metal against bone,
    and clangs out of my hand.

I scramble after it.
    The bandit does the same,
    but I get it first.

I

s
w
i
n
g

i
n

a
n

a
r
c

I hit the dirty, ugly man under his chin.
    He flies backward,
    spitting blood.

He crawls away and
    I see the other bandits also run.
    One drags my suitcase behind them.

But it's not so bad.
    A little water, a little food.
    We can do without.

It won't kill us.
    We can do without.
    What's important is we're alive.

I cheer that we've won and the rest follow me.
    Kurt whoops and Garret picks up Skye
    and swings her around.

Jaynee says we have to regroup
    and hurry away or they might attack again.
    Garret says they would be stupid to try.

That's when I see Rob on the ground, unmoving.
    That's when I hear Rowan's cries.
    That's when I realize Rob is dead.

54

Rob is dead.

Rowan's tears fall like the poison rain.

Rob is dead.

One of the bandits stuck him with a shard of glass.

Rob is dead.

His blood leaks out onto the broken concrete.

Rob is dead.

55

Rowan refuses to leave him.

Jaynee tells us that we

MUST

leave. That we

CANNOT

stay.

56

Rowan lifts up Rob,
and
when she almost drops him,
I help her.

My suitcase is gone, but Kurt takes Rowan's.

We carry Rob's body between us until it is dark.

By the time we stop, I can barely walk.

Carrying Skye is easy.
She's small and light
(and alive).

Carrying Rob is hard.
He's big and heavy
(and dead).

Rowan drags him to a ruined building.

She looks for stones,
and we all help her
(grateful we're alive).

When Rob is covered,
we all say a few words
(grateful we're not dead).

58

Jaynee says:
   "Rob was smart."

Kurt says:
   "Rob was loyal."

Garret says:
   "Rob was funny."

Skye says:
   "Rob was strong."

I say:
   "Rob was great."

Rowan says nothing. Her grief is too much.

59

The next day I'm afraid
    that Rowan won't want to leave
        Rob's grave.

Her sadness rolls off of her
    like smoke from a fire
        and is just as suffocating.

But she gets up and takes her suitcase
    and doesn't even look back
        at the gravesite.

I walk beside her in case she needs me
    and when we've walked for a while,
        she takes my hand.

I don't tell her that it will be okay
    because I don't know
        if that is a lie.

Instead I hold her hand, and
    I feel that she understands
        that we are here together.

Rob was her family,
    but now we're her
        family too.

Tears fall from her eyes,
    and she wipes them with her free hand
        and I take her suitcase from her.

So she can cry and rub her face
    and hold my hand
        at the same time.

Sometimes, just being there
    for the ones you love
        is good enough.

60

That night,
Rowan sings
a song.

It's sad
and
haunting.

That night,
I barely
sleep.

That night,
I hold Rowan
in my arms.

It's also sad
and
haunting.

<u>61</u>

Because of what happened with the bandits, Jaynee
changed some things.

We can't afford to make the same mistake again.

We take turns watching as we walk. Always watching.

Especially our backs.

Skye sits on the suitcase while Rowan and I pull it.

She can see everything behind us.

Kurt thought it was a lot to put on her. She's just a
little girl.

But we all have to help.

None of us can be useless. None of us can be
dead weight.

Or we'll end up like Rob.
We'll end up dead.

<u>62</u>

There is a place for us to stop along the way.
A place that Jaynee says is still alive
and where we can get more water.

She says it's called a waypoint
and we can rest for a day or two
then move on again.

But when we get there,
all we find is a crumbling building
and a water pump that has dried up.

There's a metal structure that
Jaynee says was a train.
"Like in the Shining City?!" Skye asks.

The thing is falling apart and rusted.
Metal teeth lay in an open, jagged mouth.
Skye wants to get on it, thinks it will take us away.

Jaynee tells Skye not to go near. That she'll get hurt.
"This is nothing like the Shining City,"
Jaynee assures her.

Beside the building, there are skeletons
covered in rotting clothes
and clutching their belongings.

One is so small, wrapped in the
bones of what was once its
mother's arms.

We don't bother to rest
in that horrible
dead place.

63

Jaynee takes me aside and tells me
that our water is low
that we must go out of our way
that we have no other choice.

On the map is a lake of fresh water, but
it might be like the waypoint
it might be dried up
it might be poison.

We have no other choice.
We have to try.

First, we get a big gulp of water (I give half to Skye).

Then we get a small mouthful of water (I pretend to drink).

Then we get splash of water (it barely wets my tongue).

Then we get a drop of water (one last drop).

Then there is no water left.

You

don't

realize

how much

you need something

until you don't have it.

I've never been this thirsty

in my entire life. All I want is

a sip of water. A drop of water.

My tongue sticks to the top of my mouth

and it hurts to swallow. I am tempted to drink

out of the puddles by the side of the road, the

poison water that will burn my mouth and rot my insides

and kill me. But I don't care. I am so thirsty. I focus

on putting one foot in front of the other. I focus

on keeping my family safe.

I focus on—

66

Nothing.

There is nothing.

Nothing.

67

I wake to water flowing into my mouth.

I gulp, grabbing at the bottle.

Then I vomit water onto the ground.

And pass out again.

"Slowly, Mal," someone says the next time I wake.
I open my eyes to a friendly face.
Rowan is there.
But where is here?

She holds a glass of water to my lips.
I swallow a few mouthfuls
and hope that it will stay in my stomach.
"Where?" I croak.

"We've made it," Rowan says.
"We're safe.
We're at Sanctuary."

69

Jaynee says that we were all in bad shape,
but I was the worst.

Garret is also in a bed.
We'd both been giving our water to Skye.

Rowan helps him too,
but mostly she stays with me.

She tells me about where we are—
the lake, the place, the people.

It sounds so good,
she must be telling stories.

There's an older woman
who checks on us all.

                            She says to call her Mama,
                                    that everybody does.

But the name
sticks in my throat.

                            Swept away with my mother,
                                 that day I lost my family.

Mama says she runs
this place,

                that we're lucky we were found when we were,
                                  that we could have died.

She studies me
like she cares,

        tells Rowan that she's glad to see a strong girl like her,
                        that she and I make a good couple.

Rowan just nods.
But my face goes red

                at the thought that this woman, Mama,
                        thinks Rowan and I are together.

Rowan holds my hand
and smiles at me.

                                  Maybe we are.

<u>71</u>

As soon as I can,
I get up.

Rowan helps me to the door,
and I step outside.

I feel as if I am
standing on a different planet.

Not this hateful Earth,
broken and full of poison.

But a beautiful place,
with blue skies and fresh air.

And a lake that stretches
farther than I can see.

Filled with clean, blue water.

We found a group of survivors
a community
a town.

Skye thinks we've reached the Shining City.

They live on a lake
and have as much water
as they can drink.

It feels too good to be true.

<u>73</u>

Garret and I were in the clinic,
a whole building just for people to go to
when they're sick.

They gave Skye some medicine
and said they would check on her cough.

They checked out everyone else too.
Weighed us and took blood and did tests.

They want to make sure we are healthy.

We must have passed because
they give us our own house.

They say we can go where we like,
but not past the old boathouse—it's unsafe.

That side of the lake hasn't been cared for.
Those houses are old. The fields are wild.

They don't want anything to happen to us.

Our house is huge,
ten times bigger
than our old room.

There's a basement and an attic,
five bedrooms,
and three bathrooms.

There's a kitchen and dining room,
a living room,
and a room just for books.

The shower is amazing.
I stand under the water,
get *clean* for the first time in forever.

I wash off the road
and the fear
and the exhaustion.

I didn't realize
how much I missed
simply being clean.

We each can have our own room.
We each can have our own bed,
but we sleep together.

We pile together
in the large living room,
on the floor.

As if we are still on the road,
huddled in the tent.
It feels safe.

75

At dinner,
> (They have a giant room where everyone eats together.)

Mama welcomes us.
> (Everyone claps.)

There are as many people as in our old apartment.
> (But not on top of each other).

They say we can stay until we recover.
> (They say drink as much water as we want.)

They say we are welcome.

<u>76</u>

Rowan and I walk around the lake,
holding hands.

She tells me she thought
I was going to die too.

Just like Rob.

She tells me that she can't imagine
life without me.

She tells me that she wants to stay.
She asks, if we can, would I stay too?

I tell her I would do anything for her.

And then we kiss.

I want to stay with Rowan forever

    lost in her wide eyes
    and her big hair
    and her long arms.

She feels like home.

This feels like home.

78

Breakfast is eggs from the chicken coop
and pancakes from the grain stores.

Lunch is a meat and vegetable bake,
thick and rich and filling.

Dinner is fresh fish and bread,
better than anything Jaynee ever baked.

All they want in exchange is for us to work
in the garden or on the lake.

79

I work in the garden
with another boy named Cal.
Mal and Cal.

We laugh as we weed.
The rich dirt
feels good between my fingers.

I swing a pickax
to break up clumps of soil.
It makes me feel strong again.

This place is full of life.
This place is full of hope.

Garret and Rowan work on the lake.
They go out on the boat
and learn how to fish.

Rowan loves the water.
She is learning to swim
and promises to teach me.

Garret learned to tie a few knots.
He practices at night,
until his hands turn rough.

They come back from their day
bright and happy.

Kurt is no good in the garden.
And the boat makes him sick.
They will have to find a different job for him.

Jaynee watches the younger kids,
while Skye plays with them.
Her face is tight and pinched.

Skye likes the other children,
but she's never dealt with her peers
and she gets into some scuffles.

She lives in fear that she will be
kicked out of the Shining City.

Jaynee assures her this isn't the Shining City,
and Jaynee will always protect her.

I can tell they aren't happy,
but they'll find their place.

<u>81</u>

The first time it rains at the lake,
we all run inside

screaming.

But nobody else does.

Slowly, we realize that somehow
the rain here isn't poison.

Somehow, this place is safe.

Somehow, this place is truly a sanctuary.

To be in the rain without fear
is the strangest thing.

To let it drip down your face
and fall on your arms

```
d           d   d           d               d
            d   d
r           r   r               r           r
            r   r
i           i   i                           i
            i   i               i
p           p   p                           p
            p   p           p
```

To open your mouth
and catch the drops on your tongue.

To live without fear
is the strangest thing.

83

Garret is the first
to move into his
own room.

He jokes that
Kurt snores
too loud.

He jokes that
Skye kicks him
in the night.

But really,
he just wants
to be alone.

84

Rowan moves next
into her own room
with her own bed
and a window that faces the lake.

In the night,
she comes and gets me
and tells me she's never slept alone
and would I please come hold her.

And I hug her,
in a giant bed,
with just the two of us,
and a window that faces the lake.

Kissing Rowan
is like breathing
the freshest air.

Kissing Rowan
is like eating
your favorite food.

Kissing Rowan
is like falling
off a cliff.

Kissing Rowan
makes my heart
jump.

Mama comes to our house
    to talk with us.

"What is this about?" Jaynee asks.
    She's warned me they might want us to move on soon.

Mama ignores Jaynee and instead
    talks to Rowan as if she's the leader.

"We've had a meeting," Mama tells us.
    She means the people of Sanctuary.

"Was I voted most handsome?" Garret asks.
    We all laugh.

"We would like you to stay," Mama tells us.
    Rowan cries out with relief.

"We'll have to talk," Jaynee says.
    Her lips are in a thin, tight line.

"Of course, you can all discuss it," Mama tells us.
    She just asks that we let her know soon.

Mama leaves us, and Rowan seems furious.
    "Why would you be rude to her?" she asks Jaynee.

"Why wouldn't we stay?" asks Kurt.
    I can't think of any reason not to.

But Jaynee takes me aside.

"Something is wrong here, Malcolm," Jaynee says.
   Her eyes see everything.

"There are not enough people to work their fields."
   Her ears hear everything.

"They don't let us go past the old boathouse. What is
back there?"
   She thinks of everything.

"I will find out," I promise her.
   All I've seen of this place is good.

"I'm sure it's just unsafe," I assure her.
   That's what I've heard.

"If it's nothing, I think we should stay," I tell her.
   I think we should stay.

87

When everyone is asleep
   in our big, safe house,
      I sneak out to the lake.

        Jaynee will feel so stupid
           when I prove her wrong.
           She's always right.

Past the old boathouse,
   there is nothing that makes
      me think anything is wrong,

        except a sound carried on the wind.
        I have to investigate
          so I can be sure.

And in a barn, I find them.
    People, tied to the walls with ropes
        like animals in a pen.

        None are well, that's easy to see.
          They are thin and have sores
            and some are just children.

When they see me,
    some hide, trying to burrow
        deeper into the filth.

        "Who are you all?" I ask,
          horrified but trying
            desperately to think of an
              explanation.

"Help me," one says
    through broken teeth,
        his voice raspy.

        "Save me," another pleads.
            "We'll leave. We won't be a drain."
                She holds a child too ill to cry.

"Kill me," begs a man,
    and the look in his eyes
        scares me more than anything.

        More than poison rain,
            more than bandits,
                more than anything.

"I'll try to help you all,"
  I promise and back away.
    Some of the people cry out,
      some scream,
        but most just stare.

  It feels like I'm lying,
    breaking a promise.
      But I have no way to free them now
      and I have to tell the others
        Sanctuary isn't what it seems.

I sneak back to our house
  and wake up Jaynee
    and tell her what I saw.

      She nods and
        I wish that Jaynee
          was not always right.

88

"They were so thin," I tell Jaynee.

They were starving.

"Except their eyes."

Wide in their shrunken faces.

"Most didn't even ask for help."

They knew no help would come.

"They'd given up on living."

They were between the living and the dead.

"Why?" I ask because Jaynee knows things.

Maybe she can explain what I saw.

"Maybe they're slaves," she says with a sigh.

Mama works them until they die.

"Maybe they're criminals."

Sanctuary doesn't want to waste food on them.

"Maybe they're..." I hold up my hand.

I don't want to hear it. I don't want to know.

She says it anyway:

"Maybe they're food."

In the morning, before breakfast, we tell everyone
what I saw.

> Jaynee says, "We have to leave. Now. Before they
> know we plan to."

> Garret says, "At least *we're* not dying of hunger."

> Kurt says, "We should ask them what's going on."

> Rowan says, "We shouldn't jump to conclusions."

> Skye says, "I like it here. I don't feel so sick."

Everyone looks at me.
Everyone wants me to say something.
Everyone wants me to decide.

In the morning, at breakfast, I can barely eat.
I pick at my eggs and wonder what meat is on my plate.
I take a bite, but the food tastes like nothing in my mouth.

Jaynee elbows me and tells me to act normal.

Skye gives one bite to herself and one to her
teddy bear.

Kurt looks as if he is about to vomit.

Rowan says we don't know anything yet.

Garret eats every scrap off his plate.

90

After breakfast,

Rowan pulls me aside
and begs me
to stay.

I can't say no to her.
But I can't say yes either.

91

I find Cal,
my new friend from the garden.

I ask him for the truth.

His smile fades
into a thin line.

"The truth is that here you are safe," he tells me, grimly.

"I saw them," I say.
 The people Sanctuary has captive.

"Who are they?"
 Those poor people.

"Why are they there?"
 There must be a reason.

I tell him that I need to know.
I don't back down.

He explains everything.

92

People come to them all the time.
They want food and water.
They want safety.

They want sanctuary.

But Sanctuary must be careful about who they accept.

The strong people stay.
They become part of the community.

The weak become livestock.
They are no longer people.

They are kept like animals.
They are fed hardly anything.

They are not given a choice.
They are forced to work the fields
until they are skin and bone.

"And then?" I ask.

Cal shrugs. "They're livestock."
   His red face and stiff shoulders tell me everything.

"But you're strong!" he says.
   "You'll be a part of the community. And your
   girlfriend. That tall girl."

"But what about Skye?" I ask.
   "She's never been strong or healthy."

Cal looks at the ground.
   "It might not be good for the other girl, and the
   short boy either."

Jaynee and Kurt.

"But you'll stay, won't you?" Cal asks. "Anything is
better than being out there."
   I tell him I need time to think.

93

I ask Jaynee why they've been so nice to us.
    They gave us food.
    They gave us water.
    Mama made us feel welcome.
Why bother, if they only want half of us?

Jaynee says that they do it to make the strong ones stay.
    They get a taste of safety.
    They get a taste of comfort.
    They get a taste of sanctuary.
Then they accept that only the strong are truly welcome.

That's why they didn't
make Jaynee and Kurt and Skye
livestock yet.

They want
me and Rowan and Garret
to love the place first.

To be happy here.
To betray our friends.

I will never give them my family.

<u>94</u>

Rowan and Garret want to stay.
Despite everything.

"They'll make them slaves," I say.
How could they betray their family?

They tell me to let Jaynee and Kurt and Skye escape.
But we can stay here.

Safe and happy.
I don't know what to say.

For the first time, I don't want to be with Rowan.
I want to be alone.

95

She finds me by the lake
and sits by my side.

Taking my hand in hers,
she tells me that she loves me.

She tells me that we can have a life here.
She tells me she can't return to the road.

She wants me to let Jaynee and the rest go.
She tries to kiss me.

I leave her there, by the lake.

The only girl I ever loved.

I leave her there, by the lake.

And I choose the unknown.

I leave my heart there, by the lake.

97

We leave that night.
Jaynee, Kurt, Skye, and I.
  Rowan and Garret would not even consider leaving.

Kurt stole water—
no one pays any attention to him.
  He filled up our plastic bottles by the lake one at
  a time.

Jaynee stole medicine—
visited the clinic, said she had a headache.
  The medicine will make Rowan and Garret sleep
  through the night.

I stole food—
from the garden and the kitchen.
  I hope I am doing the right thing.

Rowan begins to nod off after dinner and I tuck her in bed.
Jaynee put the medicine in her food and said she will
sleep through the night.

As her eyes get heavy, Rowan grabs my hand.
"I love you, Mal," she says.

"I love you too," I tell her.
She falls asleep and I kiss her forehead.

I look at her one last time
before I leave her forever.

99

Ninety-nine times out of a hundred,
I would choose Rowan.

Ninety-nine times out of a hundred,
it would be the right choice.

Ninety-nine times out of a hundred,
we would be happy together.

But this is the one time I can't choose her.
My love for Rowan isn't worth my family's freedom.

All is dark and quiet.

We take our suitcases

and our plastic wrap

and our stolen food

and flee.

"What are you doing?" Garret asks.

He isn't asleep.
The medicine didn't work on him.
Or he wasn't given enough.

"We're leaving," Jaynee tells him.

He looks hurt.
That we didn't tell him.
That we didn't say goodbye.

"You love it here," I say.

I knew he wouldn't want to leave.
I didn't want to make him choose.
I wanted it to be easy.

"This will ruin everything," he shouts.

They might not want him anymore.
They might make him livestock.
He can't believe we'd do this to him.

"I can't let you," he yells.

> There is hurt in his eyes.
> There is anger on his face.
> There is bitterness in his voice.

"Help!" he screams. "They're escaping!"

> He doesn't care that we're his family.
> He doesn't care that we love him.
> To him, we are just livestock.

We run.

102

We cut across the garden,
past the old boathouse,
to the place where
people are kept
as if they are animals.

Kurt says it's a
waste of time,
but I can't leave them
here like this,
bound and in pain.

I stole garden shears and a pickax
from the garden shed.
I cut and strike again and again,
breaking the ropes,
as many as I can.

Those that can run
do run. We follow,
hoping the people of
Sanctuary will not be able
to catch us all.

I carry Skye,
but still Jaynee and Kurt
find it hard to keep up.
Kurt falls and cuts his leg
on a piece of broken metal.

It is hours before we can rest,
and I'm sure that no one
from Sanctuary has followed us.
Skye cries and Kurt bleeds.
Jaynee looks at the map.

And I sit, alone.

103

Jaynee bandages Kurt's leg, but as we walk,
his wound reopens.

Blood seeps from the bandage and
down his leg.

He doesn't complain,
but that is somehow scarier.

A dog, or a wolf, or some other creature
howls in the distance.

"Garret…he…" Kurt can't finish. Garret betrayed us.

"He was scared," Jaynee says. "He wanted to stay."

"He could have let us go!" Kurt says. His voice is full of pain.

"He didn't mean it," Skye tells us. "He's family."

"Not anymore," I say.

105

I dream of Rowan.
I dream of what could have been.
I dream that I stayed with her.
I dream that we were happy.

But it's just a dream and I wake on the cold ground.

Kurt snores.
Skye sucks her thumb, then coughs.
Jaynee, awake, studies the map.
This is my reality.

I wish I could live in my dreams.

106

Kurt's wound won't heal, but we have to keep moving.
    Every night, the howls get louder,
    the creatures bolder.

I carry Skye on my suitcase, rolling her behind me.
    It's hard to do it on my own,
    but there's no one else who can.

The roads aren't as damaged here.
    There are still ruins and rubble, but also
    patches of green grass and skinny trees.

Jaynee helps Kurt walk and we stumble along.
    Every step brings us farther away from Rowan.
    Every step brings us closer to a place that might
    be better than where we left.

We
walk
rest
walk
sleep
walk
rest
walk
sleep
walk
rest
walk
sleep
walk
rest
walk
sleep
walk
rest
sleep
walk

108

"Help!" Kurt screams.

A large dog has him
by the leg
and is dragging him
away.

I grab a pickax
and swing it
at the dog.

But there are more
of them, a pack.
All breeds, all shapes and sizes,
all hungry.

They used to be our pets,
but they've been left alone
so long they've gone back to
being wild.

I can't fight them all.

Skye shrieks.

Jaynee grabs her and
runs away, not even
trying to help
Kurt.

Jaynee is always right,
but this doesn't seem
like the right thing
to do.

I grab as much of
our stuff as I can
and follow her.

Behind me,
Kurt wails.

His screams are cut short.

"His blood brought them," Jaynee says.
It's true.
They followed us because of him.

"There was nothing we could have done," Jaynee says.
It's true.
There were so many.

"Kurt was going to die from his wound eventually," Jaynee says.
It's true.
He wasn't healing.

"Mal, we need you," Jaynee says.
It's true.
They need me to live.

When Skye finally falls back asleep, Jaynee comes to me.

"Let me explain," she says.
She tells me that she didn't abandon Kurt. She saved Skye.

"We could run when the dogs were distracted,
or we could all stay to die."

How is that different than Garret and Rowan
wanting to stay in Sanctuary?

I don't understand.
The world used to make sense.

The earth was against us, but now we're against each other.
I'm glad that Jaynee is here to make the hard choices.

Choices I can't make on my own.
If it was all up to me, we'd all be together.

If it was all up to me, we'd all be dead.

111

Skye doesn't talk anymore.
She just stares
and coughs.

It doesn't help the air has cooled.
We can see our breath in the morning
and at night.

Her illness is back.
The medicine Jaynee stole has run out.
Skye's time has run out.

Skye is sick.
And she's not going to get better.

Her coughs shake the world.

Cough

Cough

Cough

<u>113</u>

Skye's breath rattles
in and out.

Skye's eyes flutter
open and closed.

Skye drifts between
awake and asleep.

Skye hovers between
alive and dead.

114

Still I carry her.
Still I carry on.

<u>115</u>

One morning, Jaynee tells me
that we can't move Skye.

So, we sit with her and watch her
breathe her last breath.

And when she is still,
her eyes open and unseeing,

Jaynee and I cry over her body
for everything we've lost.

I dig a grave on the side of the road,
small for her small body.

I place Skye in the hole and
Jaynee and I use our hands to bury her with dirt.

We mark her grave with her purple teddy bear
she carried all this way.

We leave her our love, too—it's all we have to give.
Then we continue walking down the road.

116

It's just me and Jaynee again, like that day of the flood
when my other family was washed away.

"Do you remember," she asks, "when we met?"
It's like she read my mind.

But Jaynee knows things.
She even knows what I'm thinking.

I sit down on the road.
"I don't want to go on," I tell her.

"What is the point?" I ask.
Tia left us. We couldn't save Kurt or Skye.

Garret betrayed us.
Rowan is lost to me forever.

"We should just give up," I say, my head in my hands.

She sits next to me, and starts to tell me the
story of the Shining City.

117

Once upon a time,
there was a Shining City by a lake.

The lake was clear and pure,
and healthy fish swam in its waters.

"I don't want to hear that story," I tell her.
It makes me think of our cozy apartment.

It makes me think of my family
gathered comfortably around a candle.

It makes me think of better times,
and right now, I don't want to think about anything.

"It's not a story," Jaynee tells me.
"It's the truth."

I look at her, unbelieving.
"The little girl in the story is me," she tells me.

"I was born in the Shining City," she tells me.
It's all real. She grew up there. And that's where we're going.

She tells me the story of the Shining City,
and this time she tells the whole truth.

Everything I told you about the Shining City was true.
  There are thousands of electric lights
  and trains that rush across the land.

There are buildings that can withstand storms,
  domes that keep the rays of the sun
  from burning your skin like fire in summertime.

They take care of the lake, which is clear and blue.
  The fish in it aren't rotting or poison.
  It's so large you can't see the other edge.

"Just like Sanctuary," I interrupt.
    Skye had thought we'd found our Shining City.
    I had too.

"It's nothing like Sanctuary," she tells me.
    The people have to work, sure,
    but they aren't slaves.

"People there are free," she tells me.
    She continues her story
    with a desperate tone.

My father and mother broke the law.
  People in the Shining City are free,
  but there are still rules, still law.

They were forced out of the city.
  We traveled south. We found a place on the water.
  But then the floods came.

That's when I met you.
  Both our families had been washed away.
  So, we made a new family.

"What did your parents do…?" I pause.
 Does she even know?
 Does it even matter?

"The point is, if we make it, they'll take us in."
 They take in refugees,
 but you have to follow the rules.

"You were just waiting this whole time to go back?" I ask.
 She nods. We needed supplies,
 and a strong enough family.

"Why didn't you tell me this was *real*?" I ask.
 She knows it's too good to be true.
 She thought we wouldn't believe her.

<u>119</u>

I stand and help her up.
I wipe my hands on my plastic-covered pants.

"Let's go," I say.
"Let's go to the Shining City."

"I wanted us all to make it," she tells me.
"I wanted Skye to see it.

"We'll make it for them," I say.
We'll see it for them all.

<u>120</u>

Jaynee shows me how to read the map properly.

We still have a long way to go, but without Skye, we move faster.

I hate myself for thinking that we're better off.

I hate that I think she might be better off.

<u>121</u>

The rain comes down
    in a sheet of poison water
        and I'm not fast enough.

I get some on my hands.
    My skin grows red and irritated.
        Little blisters form on my fingers.

Jaynee uses our precious fresh water to rinse them off.
    It is painful, and Jaynee tries to distract me.
        She feeds me peanut butter and chocolate.

It rains for two days straight and we are stuck in the tent.
　　It's awkward when we have to pee in an empty bottle,
　　　　but we close our eyes when the other person goes.

We talk about the families we lost.
　　I didn't realize how much I remembered about
　　　　my parents and my little sister.

I remember my dad loved to dance,
　　and my mom loved to sing,
　　　　and my sister was scared of hurricanes.

Jaynee had two brothers, one older and one younger.
  She ran with them and fought with them
      and bossed them around.

We talk about the people we lost.
  Tia, who wouldn't leave the place she knew.
      Kurt, always afraid, but also always brave.

We talk about Garret and Rowan and hope they're happy.
  And we talk about Skye, so weak.
      Maybe she's happy someplace too now.

122

Finally, the rain stops and we can move on.

I fold up the tent and Jaynee gasps.

Afraid, I whirl around, but there's no danger.

Instead there's a rainbow.

Jaynee cries for the first time since I've known her.

I watch her tears fall down like rain.

<u>123</u>

As we walk, Jaynee tells me about the past:

    She tells me that people treated the world badly.

    She tells me that's when our world broke.

    She tells me that's why the rain is poison.

    She tells me that's why so many people have died.

As we walk, Jaynee tells me about the Shining City:

    She tells me about basketball.

    She tells me about ice cream.

    She tells me about television.

    She tells me about shopping malls.

<u>124</u>

I ask questions too, now that I know the Shining City
is real.

How will we know when we're close?

> We'll see the city's light in the night sky.
> And the air will get cooler.
> And the road will be easier.

Will there be more people?

> There will, but they won't be desperate.
> They won't try to hurt us.
> They might try to help us.

How is the lake not poison?

> She says that is one way that the
> Shining City is like Sanctuary.
> The rain is fresh and pure.

When will we get there?

> Any day now.
> We are so close.
> Any day now.

125

It rains again and we wait in the tent as the water falls

d
o
w
n

d
o
w
n

d
o
w
n

Jaynee has an odd look on her face.
　　She darts her hand out of the tent and squeals.

"What are you doing?" I yell.
　　We don't have fresh water to waste.

She looks at her hand and screams,
　　but it's a happy scream.

She holds out her hand to me.
　　There are no blisters. No redness.

The rain is fresh.

I hoot and hug her,
    then I run outside and catch the rain in my mouth.

We jump in puddles and splash each other.
    I peel off the plastic I wear and let the rain wash
    over me.

We are so close to the Shining City.
    And now we can travel while it storms.

We don't have to hide from the poison rain.
    I feel like nothing can stop us.

<u>127</u>

Jaynee makes me put the plastic back on.
She says it will be hard to walk in the rain.

She's right. I'm wet and cold.
My feet are rubbed raw.

The rain doesn't let up.
It gathers in a stream at our feet.

Our tent would have washed away.
What we need is a boat.

The stream becomes a river,
and still it rains.

"There!" Jaynee shouts,
and points to an abandoned house.

We make our way slowly to it
and push inside.

The wood is old and rotted,
but we climb up the old stairs to the second floor.

It's not the best place,
but it's out of the rain.

We'll stay until the storm passes
and we can continue on.

Lightning flashes and thunder cracks,
making me jump.

I laugh and turn to find Jaynee smiling too.
Then the floor disappears.

128

I am dragged into the churning water,

    tossed and thrown.

It pulls me under and I hit a wall—

    first my shoulder, then my head.

Black spots dot my eyes and if I don't get a breath of air,

    I will gulp water into my lungs.

I hit the wall again, and then I'm through it,

    carried along with the river of water.

My head comes above the water line

and I gasp for air.

I go back under, my eyes searching

for any sign of Jaynee.

My feet hit the ground and I kick up

with all my might.

Another panicked breath and another

before I'm swept away again.

129

I catch hold of a plank and
    though I'm exhausted,
        I hang on for dear life.

I shift myself on the board
    so it supports my weight
        and I catch my breath.

I scream for Jaynee
    until my throat is sore
        and no sound comes out.

I ride the plank of wood
    down the flooding water
        at the river's mercy.

130

I wash up on higher ground and crawl to safety.

The rain has let up.

I make myself walk back the way that I came.

I make myself look for Jaynee.

131

I find Jaynee,
    cold and blue-lipped.

I sit next to her
    and pick the leaves out of her hair.

Jaynee who knew so much
    now knows nothing.

Jaynee who said so much
    will now be silent forever.

132

My family all died, so long ago in a flood.
    Now the last of my family has also drowned.

I lost everything, so I dig her grave with my fingers
    and place her in the shallow hole.

I am the only one left.

I am alone in the world.

133

I had the map last, and it is still tucked into my pocket.
I pull it out, soaked, but I can't figure out where I am.

I walk along the draining waters until I find a sign,
old and creaking.

Then I walk along the road,
feeling like the flash flood washed away who I was.

Who am I now
without my family?

At night, the temperature drops.
I can see my breath in the air.

Still I walk. If I stop, I will die.
I walk until dawn comes, then I keep walking more.

I have no food. I drink water from puddles
on the side of the road.

Still I walk.
Still I walk.
Still I walk.

Sometimes I think
that Jaynee made up
the Shining City.

Sometimes I think
that I made up
my family.

Sometimes I think
that I made up
Rowan.

Sometimes I think
that I made up
everything but me.

135

At one point,
    during the never-ending day,
        I fall over.

I lay there
    in a fitful haze
        that could be called sleep.

I dream that I am back home
    and everyone surrounds me—
        Tia, Garret, Kurt, Rob, Rowan, Jaynee, and Skye.

We are happy and warm in my dream,
    but when I wake, I am lying facedown
        in the road.

I was never the smart one

or the funny one

or the sensitive one

or the strong one

or the weak one.

I'm just me.

But maybe...
I'm the one who survives.

Maybe that's enough.

So I stand and do what I do best—

I keep moving forward.

136

That night,
in the darkness,
I see it.

In the distance,
something
glows.

I jog,
then run
toward it.

Bright
and inviting
and safe.

I have reached the Shining City.

WANT TO KEEP READING?

If you liked this book, check out another book
from West 44 Books:

THE VANISHING PLACE
BY THERESA EMMINIZER

ISBN: 9781538385081

It Started

with a *yes*.

A *yes*
that slipped
easily
from my lips.

*Would you girls want to
      meet up later?*

        *We could all go out
on Nate's dad's boat?*

Jay's green eyes
were both
        nervous and eager.

His voice was
low and soft.

        Like the moon

                s u s p e n d e d

        over the water.

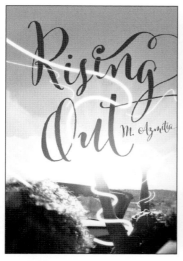

CHECK OUT MORE BOOKS AT:
www.west44books.com

An imprint of Enslow Publishing

WEST **44** BOOKS™

ABOUT THE AUTHOR

Demitria Lunetta is the author of many YA books including **THE FADE, BAD BLOOD,** and the sci-fi duology, **IN THE AFTER** and **IN THE END. OUR BROKEN EARTH** is her second hi-lo book and her first novel in verse. BITTER & SWEET is her first hi-lo book and also available from West 44 Books. Find her on Twitter, Facebook, and at demitrialunetta.com.